Published in Great Britain in 2021 by Matthew Cash Burdizzo

Books Walsall, UK

WERWOLF

MATTHEW CASH

BURDIZZO BOOKS 2021

For Kirsty
Matty-Bo
xxx

1.

Their boots crunched on fresh snow; Lieberman wished to Christ he had worn another pair of socks.

The rest of the troop jogged ahead through the woodland, heavy equipment rattling against their backs.

The trail had been hard to find, it would have been completely impossible if they weren't able to persuade the farmer to show them the way.

Liebermann was a master at persuasion, it was an understatement for what he did to convince the farmer.

He had the farmer's wife and daughter stripped bare; guns pressed against their temples hard enough to break the skin. His men looked with uncomfortable arousal.

They would do whatever they were told.

Fortunately the situation didn't escalate from the threat of what they would do, the farmer saw no choice than provide an escort through the woods to show what he had found.

Liebermann lit a cigarette and squinted up at the sun.

The word was the British were winning the war, the Fuhrer would be beaten, but Liebermann had faith in his country's army, his country's leader. And if what was rumoured to be here was fact, as fantastical as it seemed, it could be the answer to their prayers for victory.

Werewolves were a thing of myth and legend, fairy stories to frighten at Christmas. But after the first platoon of men went missing he had to know if this was fact or fiction.

Every avenue must be investigated

A soldier pointed to the farmer who showed them all a rifle he found.

Liebermann passed his men to examine it. It was German-issued and a soldier knew better than to leave his weapon. He passed it to the nearest man who slung it over his shoulder.

"How much further, farmer?" Liebermann spat at the stocky man that led them.

The farmer muttered something quietly, fear evident on his ruddy cheeks.

He pointed at something through the trees.

Through the trunks, blackened against the stark of the snow, Liebermann saw a small wooden building.

He moved his men closer.

A chalet, Swiss-style here in the middle of the forest was unusual. Smoke coiled up from a central chimney, one wall of the two-storey building was half-covered in a log stack. A small shed sat to the left of the house; gutted rabbits hung from the eaves.

Liebermann signalled his men to keep low as they took a moment to watch.

They rested. They took the opportunity to eat and drink, soothe their feet and lay their heavy packs and weaponry down.

The front door of the chalet opened and a huge bear of a man stepped out.

Liebermann estimated the man was close to seven-foot. A long red shaggy beard covered his broad barrel chest. He wore a fur deerstalker over long red hair and an ill-fitted German military Parka. Further evidence that this man was part of what the farmer feared. Liebermann didn't believe this wild man killed a troop of German soldiers.

He couldn't be alone, this man, there was no way he could fight a platoon of armed soldiers, no matter how much of a hulk he was.

The bear reached back into the darkness of the house and brought out a long-handled axe.

Jesus, Liebermann thought looking at the wood stacked up beside the house, how much wood did they need?

"Schneider, Grueller, Schmidt, take him and do it quickly and quietly." The three soldiers nodded and despite their feelings of doubt crept through the snowy foliage.

Liebermann watched as the giant grabbed a four-foot-long section of tree trunk and went to work splitting it with the axe and a grunt.

His men kept low, their bayonets drawn and when they broke the cover of trees they ran silently towards the man's back.

The snow muffled most noise and before the man had a chance to hear the crunch of their boots, they were on him.

Schmidt thrust his blade into the man's kidneys and he let out a roar that was more animal than human. With the knife embedded in his side, he swung the axe around and in one fluid motion separated Schneider's legs from his torso whilst he ran back to Liebermann. He changed the axe's trajectory and cleaved off the front of Grueller's head. Grueller's halved brain slopped from the skull as his body crumpled.

Schmidt shrieked and turned back towards his comrades, his face bespeckled with the gore of his fallen companions.

The giant swung the axe again and cut through Schmidt's back as he ran, severing his spine and sending him flying forwards to die slowly in the snow.

The giant yanked the bayonet from his side and roared. His angry red face pointed at the yellow blot in the sky like he had some age-old vendetta. His rage turned animalistic and he changed into something bigger, fiercer.

Liebermann shouted for his men to attack and within ten seconds they were all up and running. He drew his handgun and sped towards the chalet. "Hold him off whilst Fischer gets ready."

The bear of a man tore away his clothing to allow his metamorphosis, the platoon peppered him with bullets. The ammunition did nothing other than slow his movements as they approached.

Liebermann stared in wonder at the beast, it towered above his men, at least nine feet tall. A wolf's head four times the size of the generic animal salivated on the shoulders of a herculean torso. It was covered in coarse fur that faded from red to grey, its hands both human and animal, with sickle sized claws where fingernails should be. It raked a bunch of those claws across one of his men's faces and the strings of flesh blinded the man to his side.

It was going to take more firepower to bring this monster down. Liebermann turned to another of his men, Fischer.

Fischer strode towards his superior decked from head to toe in his black fireproof gear. A fuel tank was strapped to his back, a gun-like nozzle held out in front of him, a small flame flickered from the end waiting for him to shoot napalm.

Over the gunfire they heard screams come from inside the chalet.

A middle-aged woman exited the doorway; her own clothes ripped as her own rapid transformation began.

Liebermann saw shapes of two children behind her, safe in the confines of the house.

Safe. For now.

He turned and fled into the woods.

The husband-and-wife werewolf team tore their way through his men easily but they held them off for Fischer to get them with the flamethrower.

He squeezed the trigger and directed a spray of flame at the male monster's chest. He roared in agony as he was engulfed in fire.

The female monster increased her attack anew cutting and shearing her way through Liebermann's men, her husband tried to put out the flames by rolling on the snow and the fleeing soldiers. Fischer swept the flame towards her shouting at the men to move.

A voice yelled over the cacophony, "Halt!"

At the sound of their leader's voice the remaining soldiers backed away from the husband and wife forsaking any of their fallen comrades for their own safety.

The male monster ceased rolling around in the snow. The fire extinguished, his fur charred and blackened; open wounds bubbled and seeped.

The female stood snarling at the fleeing soldiers before turning to Liebermann.

The shock of what she saw defeated the animal within her and the mother inside overwhelmed her.

Her transformation back to a woman was fluid and she huddled naked in the snow.

The father sat up on his elbows, Fischer's nozzle pointed at his blistered head.

All eyes looked to Liebermann.

Liebermann stood in the doorway to the chalet, a small snarling boy in a headlock, his pistol pressed against his temple. Beside him was a girl, the boy's double, she trembled in a puddle of her own urine. "Now I have your undivided attention. I expect you to listen."

The children's parents looked mournfully at the man holding their children, worried at their son's ferocious struggles.

"Be still, Sebastian," the father called out, his voice hoarse and distorted due to burnt vocal cords.

The boy obeyed his father.

Liebermann saw the father's wounds healing, it was miraculous, but there was no doubt that these things felt pain. He nodded to the gun and spoke to the father, "Now, I'm not sure if this would have any permanent effect on your son. But I am certain, going by your own reactions to knife and flame, that a bullet, at this proximity, going through your son's head would most definitely cause damage, and definitely hurt. The beauty of your remarkable -" Liebermann paused and stared serenely at the treetops, searching for the right word, "- condition is that I could do this over and over again, why, you would be a torturer's dream subject."

The look of defeat in the father's eyes reflected in the mother's sobbing submission.

2.

Victor straightened the knot of his black tie and checked his hair was neatly groomed. He turned to the lady in the leather armchair on the other side of the room. Her grey hair had grown long, he could never get it looking pristine like she had in her own time.

He would have to ask, yet again, for the use of a hairdresser.

"You must finish your coffee Gwen before it gets cold." Victor picked up a black cane and strode across the carpet to his wife's side.

His wife stared across the room with a delirious grin, "Oh look, Victor, isn't it beautiful?"

Victor agreed warmly, having no idea where his wife was mentally, somewhere in the past, a happy occasion this time, which was a blessing.

He raised a cup to his wife's lips and sighed as she slurped at the lukewarm coffee.

She looked coyly at a decade's younger version of her husband and laughed with mischief, "oh Victor, wine this early in the day, what would mother say?"

"Ah," Victor said humouring her delusion.

He guessed she was reliving some happy time shared between the two of them. By what she was saying he suspected it was their honeymoon.

"Are we celebrating?"

They had been married for seventy years, had only ever known one another.

She served him as his dutiful wife for most of those seven decades, encouraging him throughout his career, comforting him at the lesser successful times. It went without question that he would care for her when she began to show the initial signs of dementia. It was frustrating at times, lonely too, heart-breaking, but inside the disintegrating body was the young, vibrant, intelligent lady he had fallen in love with. Her moments of clarity were rare these days but he would care for her whilst he still could.

Victor picked up a book and lowered himself into a matching armchair adjacent to Gwen's. He pulled a sleek gold pen from his suit jacket pocket and scribbled onto a page.

A heavy series of knocks rapped on the door to his lounge, Victor closed the book and glanced across the room, "Enter."

The door swung open and a tall man entered the room.

He had dark blonde hair that was greased into position and a freshly groomed short beard. His right arm shot out and up, palm flattened, "Heil Hitler!"

"Heil, mein Führer. Bertram, what brings you here this evening?" Victor offered a puny imitation of Liebermann's salute. He suspected that yet again it was to report another failed mission, a wild goose chase.

Liebermann strode into the room; Gwen still sat beaming at the mantlepiece, lost in time. "I am here Victor, to report our success."

Victor's eyes widened, his voice trembled when he spoke, "You mean?"

Bertram Liebermann nodded smugly, "today, my troop captured a family of suspected lycanthropes."

"My God!" Victor whispered, he couldn't believe it was true, there must be some mistake.

The Nazi seemed to guess what he was thinking, "We witnessed the mother and father change into the beasts before our very eyes. We suffered many fatalities, but we persuaded them to surrender. I found their children."

"Children?" Victor gasped.

He and Gwen had never had them but he could understand how children would be a weakness to any loving parent.

"Yes, a boy and a girl, twins I believe. Seven-years-old," Liebermann examined a photograph above Victor's fireplace.

"Don't fret, the children are not harmed."

"And the parents?"

Liebermann smirked, "They are willing to comply, whatever wounds they have suffered are healing or have already."

Victor grabbed his cane and rose slowly to his feet. "Take me to them. Send someone to sit with Mrs Krauss please, sir."

Liebermann nodded and waved towards the door, "As you wish Dr Krauss."

3.

Victor's excitement was laced with more than fear. As Liebermann and his man unfastened the bolts and locks on the heavy iron door he turned to the younger German for reassurance. "You are sure that they are suitably restrained?"

Liebermann nodded, "Of course Doctor, the family is separated, the parents will do whatever we want them to. The father proved reluctant at first but I had some men demonstrate the repercussions of any unwarranted actions."

"Who are we seeing first?" Victor asked.

Liebermann pushed open the door to reveal a spacious, grey walled room.

A giant of a man slumped against a wall, ragged clothing which hung in charred tatters did little to keep his decency. He raised his head wearily at the men, he was crestfallen. His wrists and ankles were wrapped in thick chains.

"Herr Schäfer," Liebermann bellowed, "may I present to you my colleague, Doctor Victor Krauss."

The man sat expressionlessly.

Liebermann smiled and told his man to find Victor a chair. The man vanished from the room for a moment and returned moments later.

Victor dragged the chair closer to the red-haired man. It was impossible to believe that the man had suffered assault by a flamethrower earlier that day.

"You will find Herr Schäfer most cooperative Doctor," Liebermann said staring hard into Schäfer's eyes, "he knows what happens if he harms anyone."

Schäfer spat at Liebermann's boots, "You and your men raped my wife."

Victor scowled at Liebermann, "Monster."

Liebermann laughed, "That may well be, but he is the only monster that you are here to question, Doctor." He turned back to Schäfer, "Comply with the Doctor here and the same won't happen to your children."

"Leave us," Victor asked Liebermann.

Liebermann and his man left the cell.

Victor took out his notebook and pen and smiled at Schäfer, "Please, Mr Schäfer, it is best if you just answer my questions. You have seen what they will do if you don't, and I am sorry for what they have already done."

Schäfer said nothing.

Victor scanned a sheet of paper Liebermann gave him, "Now this says your name is Christoph Schäfer and," Victor paused to do quick mathematics in his head, "You were born over one hundred and fifty years ago?"

Schäfer nodded.

"Remarkable," Victor said studying the man who only physically looked to be in his thirties. "Have you always been...," he couldn't believe he was going to say this seriously, "a werewolf?"

Christoph Schäfer nodded, "I am lycan."

Victor scratched his pen across the page of his journal, spidery handwriting, barely legible. "Have you always been this way? It hasn't been passed on to you by some virus or contagion?"

Schäfer scooted backwards to sit against the wall and frustrated by the chains binding him yanked at them and beat his fists. "Are these chains necessary, doctor?"

Victor eyed him suspiciously, "Yes, for the time being. Continue to show compliance then I will see what I can do to make you comfortable. Now, please, Herr Schäfer, stop avoiding my question."

Christoph Schäfer banged his head on the cold grey bricks, he had known every inch of the room within ten minutes of being imprisoned there, just one entrance and exit, the heavily guarded iron door.

Even if there was a way out there was no point in attempting escape.

He saw first-hand what these bastards would do if he rebelled.

Liebermann had a dozen men drag him into the room, flamethrowers pointed in the faces of his children. They lashed the chains and cuffs around his wrists and ankles and beat the hell out of him with fist, boot and gunbutt.

Any sign of changing into something else from either him or his wife and their children would pay.

After Liebermann's men had quenched their bloodlust on an indestructible victim, they did the same to his wife. But Agatha, his wife, was a vision of beauty: raven-haired, curvaceous and pale-skinned. It wasn't long before Liebermann noticed the first signs of arousal in his men, leering faces at her torn clothes, her exposed flesh.

Liebermann was the first, he threw her to the floor, mashed her pretty face into the concrete as he violated her, smiling, laughing and staring into Christoph Schäfer's eyes with every thrust.

Their children hid their eyes, they allowed them that much, but he was forced to watch as one by one each of Liebermann's men took Agatha by force, no hole left unfilled. Then Liebermann's words, as his last soldier grunted his climax and punched several teeth from his wife's mouth, "Do as we ask or your children will be next."

In the space of a few hours his bruises almost healed, the lycanthropy's regeneration restored him to peak condition, but there were some parts that it couldn't reach.

"I was born with lycanthropy, we all were, true lycanthropy is hereditary." Schäfer began.

Victor made his notes. "Is that the only way this condition can be replicated?"

Schäfer shook his head, "No, but it is the only kind that doesn't turn people into blood-crazed monsters."

"How else can it be transferred?"

"By bite or blood."

"It can be spread through ingesting saliva and blood?" Victor wanted confirmation. "What about if you were to have sex with a normal woman?"

Schäfer closed his eyes against the imagery which that sentence conjured, "Then there would be a likelihood of her having lycanthrope offspring."

"And would your condition be passed on to the mother?"

"I don't know. It is unlikely but possible."

"What makes true lycanthropy different to the strain passed on via bite or by blood?"

It was obvious to Schäfer what these bastards wanted, the childlike glimmer of excitement on the old doctor's face when he said it could be passed on told him everything.

The Nazis would attempt anything to win this war. No matter how fantastical or unlikely the chance, these bastards would investigate any avenues that might make them invincible.

"A true lycan is born with this, he grows with his wolf, as the baby becomes a child he knows what he is. The wolf inside is born subservient, knows the body it inhabits is special, loves and respects its owner. It is obedient, faithful like a dog that sits by its owner's feet. The child has total control, even at the times when the moon is full and the wolf at his most insistent. The true lycan respects the wolf, feeds, nurtures him, let's him out to play regularly but keeps him on a leash, always stays in charge."

Victor scribbled Schäfer's words in longhand, making notes at how proud he seemed describing his condition. "And the infected lycan?"

Schäfer laughed coldly, "It is like trapping a tiger inside your skull. A wild animal that wants nothing but its own way. It will loathe its habitat and do whatever it can to escape it. And the only chance it has for escape is by transforming its host into its likeness, but it is only momentary and this enrages the beast. All wants is bloody death to everything in its path and will continue to fight to be the chief occupant of the host's body. Any weakness will give it control. A mental fight for control of your own body."

Victor considered Schäfer's words. "Does it have your other abilities? Regeneration?"

"Oh yes. It will come with all the goods included, the benefits of lycanthropy, it will change the host to its best physical ability, strengthen, maybe even rebuild parts that no longer work. But it will only improve things to benefit itself and it will always be in control."

Victor closed his journal and put his pen away. "Like any animal, or psychological disorder of the mind I have a theory that it can be controlled, Herr Schäfer, and I want you to help me find out how."

He touched his cane to the ground and pushed himself to his feet before backing away a few steps. "But, if you will, a demonstration. Let me see this beast inside you."

Schäfer stood mournfully, he towered above the frail, but intelligent old man, "Doctor, you know nothing."

He began to change.

When Liebermann saw the thin, bent bird-like figure of Doctor Krauss in his black suit through the iron door's grill gazing at the monstrosity five times bigger than him he swore. He barged into the room gesturing for a nearby guard to accompany him.

Victor and the wolf turned towards them.

"Go," Victor bellowed across the room like a headmaster disciplining his pupils.

Liebermann seethed but did as instructed.

4

"And after that, I shall see the children," Victor said softly as he poured the last spoonful of soup into Gwen's mouth, handkerchief ready to dab any residue. He saw it, a slight flicker in her eyes when he mentioned *children*.

They never had children even though they tried. Neither of them found out who was to blame, who the infertile one was.

It didn't matter.

The consolation of having descendants would be someone other than the government getting their belongings and money.

"Oh, Victor look," Gwen said, her usual repetitive cheerful way, "isn't it beautiful?"

Victor moved from his wife; he placed the dirty soup dish in the sink in a small kitchenette attached to their living area. "Hilda will be here any time to do your hair whilst I go do my work."

He already told her several times but knew she didn't listen to a thing he said.

He gathered his journal and walking stick and left his wife staring off into the past.

Victor pressed a hand against another iron door and glanced through the spy hole.

A girl lay on a mattress on a metal frame. Coarse filthy-looking sheets lay crumpled in a heap on the floor. She sat on the bed, her knees pressed into her chest, her head resting on them, her face hidden by long hair, red like her father's. A metal bucket, half full of urine and faeces, was the only other thing in the room.

Victor hissed with disapproval at the conditions they were keeping the child in.

Liebermann smirked at him, "The children have beds and a toilet, and I keep my men away from her. What more do you want or expect?"

"Some humanity?" Victor suggested.

Liebermann laughed and patted him on the shoulder. "That is rich coming from the man who has just drained a full-grown man of almost his entire blood supply to record his healing processes."

"I am just following orders like I have a choice in the matter?"

"We all have choices, Victor," Liebermann said as he unlocked the door. "Do or die, you need to remember what side you are on. We will go to any measures to win this war, any measures. If you are lucky you and your decrepit old wife will have played a part in our Führer's victory."

"How dare you?" Victor snapped.

Liebermann span, startling the old man, "Be about your work, Doctor, lest I send one of my men with a more senior taste to check on your wife."

Victor backed into the room, mouth agape at Liebermann's subtle threat.

For a moment he faced the closed cell door, but a ruffle of material made him turn.

The girl had moved, one of the grey sheets from the floor now wrapped her head and shoulders.

As there was no other furniture Victor stepped over to the bed and stood before the girl. "Madam, may I please sit on that uncomfortable looking contraption? I am ninety years old and my legs feel twice that."

The girl's frightened eyes flicked at him for a millisecond and then she scooted over the bed.

Victor sat down on the creaking bed and made an exaggerated *ahhh*.

The girl pulled the blanket around tighter so only her filthy face stuck out. Endless crying had cleaned streaks in the grime on her cheeks.

Victor kept silent allowing himself and the girl to get used to one another's presence.

She trembled with cold, fright or a combination of both.

"I understand that you are going through probably the most frightening time in your life." Victor began with a sad sigh, "I don't know how much of outside news and information got through to your family, how cut off you were, but I'm sure you have seen for yourself that these are not men to disobey."

The girl rolled her towards him, her forehead rested against her knee, "They did bad things to my mother." As if by just saying those words more tears flowed.

Victor felt the prickle of his own as he pitied the young girl.

With each wracking sob, short grey hairs sprung out in clusters on her cheeks but retreated as fast as they grew.

The scientist in him was fascinated.

"As long as you do as they say then no harm will come to any of you. We just want information, to know how you can do what you do, what makes you different from normal people."

The girl sniffed snot and quickly wiped away the tears on the blanket. "But we are normal people." She paused. "We just have an animal inside us which helps us. We never hurt anyone, unless they hurt us first."

"What is your name?"

"Gretchen." The girl grimaced. "I hate it."

Victor laughed, the girl was relaxing, albeit only slightly, "So, what would you prefer to be called, Snow White?"

The girl whispered, "Esmeralda."

Victor chuckled, "I haven't heard that name for a while. Is there a reason as to why Esmeralda?"

Gretchen nodded. "I like the Hunchback of Notre Dame."

"Ah, now we are on familiar territory. Victor Hugo. Well, shall I tell you something, Gretchen?" He never waited for an answer, "My name is also Victor, and I too detest my bloody name."

A small smirk lit her face.

"So, I'll do a deal with you. If you agree to talk to me, I'll refer to you only as Esmeralda. On one condition."

Gretchen's blue eyes squinted with suspicion.

"And that's if you call me Quasimodo," Victor said and squeezed one eye closed and pulled a funny face.

The girl smiled and nodded.

"So, tell me how you and your family spend your days."

Gretchen sat and concentrated on a spot on the floor, "Mother usually teaches us from books, Father does the outside chores, hunting, woodcutting. At night," She smiled in reminiscence, "At night we let our wolves out to play."

Victor leafed through the pages of his journal.

Pages of unintelligible handwriting flicked by, diagrams and a sketch of what Gretchen thought was her father. She placed her fingers on the page.

"And what games do you play?"

Hand still resting on the sketch of her father Gretchen's blue eyes bore into Victor's. "We let our wolves out to do what they do. Like domesticated dogs, they need exercise, feeding and prefer their food still living," she said it with such innocence but still, it instilled fear in the old German.

Victor's expression must have been readable as she added without haste, "But we only hunt deer. And we run, run and run."

Victor didn't take his eyes off the girl but knew what sketches she rested her hand on.

An ink drawing in black of a large bearded man, diagrams of his transformation into a werewolf. A close-up, his hand and comparisons between that and his wolf's paw.

"You have seen my father's wolf?" Gretchen asked, the question rhetorical, her previous barriers slipped back in place as she removed her hand from Victor's journal and retreated into the confines of the grey blanket.

"Yes, Lady Esmerelda, as I said earlier, we want to learn all about you, and your kind." Victor closed the book.

Gretchen said nothing, she gave a grim nod and lay on the mattress, swaddled in the blanket.

5.

Victor studied the photograph.

Christoph Schäfer strapped to a metal gurney, his abdomen opened wide. They were remarkably resilient creatures.

Under Liebermann's orders, he ran these barbaric experiments, albeit reluctantly.

Aside from anomalies in the father's blood, there was nothing to see.

Over the weeks that he poked and prodded there was nothing to explain the werewolf gene.

The last few days began to take its toll, he felt like he was getting nowhere.

He was up until the early hours trawling through notes in his journal looking at the results of the experiments and interviews recorded with all four family members.

There were no answers.

One thing he learned through Christoph was it was indeed possible for a person infected by one of the so-called *'true Lycan's* bites to overcome and therefore overpower the beast within.

It was possible to thwart its urges for control of its host.

As yet there were no scientific explanation why standard wolves howl at the moon, other than they were largely nocturnal. It was purely coincidence; that the werewolf had a similar connection to the moon was strange. In theory, if an infected victim was mentally prepared and strong enough to resist the presence inside the overwhelming urges would surface at the first full moon after being bitten, then he would be able to have control over the beast.

Victor insisted his notes and any samples were kept by him alone. Liebermann agreed but kept him under close supervision. The Nazi knew he was on the cusp of figuring out the creatures' secrets and wanted to be the one who took the credit for the first werewolf trials.

Victor hated the idea, an army of monsters tearing through the innocents, but there was nothing he could do. Though he knew there was a slim chance Liebermann would let the family go, he hoped there would be some humane way to dispose of them.

Last week Liebermann came to him with his latest morbid challenge; *to find out their weaknesses, to, if at all possible, kill Christoph Schäfer.*

It was an arduous task, physically and mentally, blood loss, poisons, suffocation, even a bullet to the brain, nothing would kill the man. Fire harmed them but their regeneration healed them as quicker than they burned. It would take prolonged exposure to incredible heat for that to have any effect.

The worst thing about it, no matter how resilient they were, was that they felt the pain of what he did. It was pointless and the only place left was the only area he hadn't investigated.

The brain.

He didn't have the knowledge or equipment to operate on a human brain, let alone this man's. Victor was stalling. He knew how devastating it would be to let this power fall into the Nazis' hands.

Liebermann wanted to know how to kill them, *needed to know*, the only thing left for Victor was dismemberment.

There was nothing else left and though he didn't want to put this man through any more suffering he knew someone else would do it if he didn't. He also knew what would happen to him and Gwen if he didn't follow orders, and he knew, although it sickened him, the scientist inside of him wanted answers to this miraculous mutation.

Victor made an accidental breakthrough in the days preceding Christoph Schäfer's execution.

He found their weakness.

Sebastian Schäfer, the son, told him about the grandfather.

6.

Sebastian Schäfer was a fighter like his father. He was kept heavily restrained since his arrival, his wolf was rampant and appeared numerous times a day.

Thick open welts oozed on his wrists and ankles from where he fought against the metal cuffs.

Blood caked his mouth where his werewolf fangs repeatedly burst through his ever-healing lips and gums each time aggression took over.

Victor knew he couldn't break free and so did the boy, but he never gave up trying.

Using Liebermann's men, Victor managed to administer different types and strengths of sedation to the boy until he found a mixture that subdued him enough for him to give up the physical fight. Victor wondered whether the boy had other issues, queried schizophrenia and so similarly medicated him.

The boy lay on a metal frame much like his sister. Drool pooled and dribbled from the corner of his mouth, his eyes widened when Victor approached.

"Grandfather?" the boy was delirious despite having met Victor numerous times. "You have come to take us? Then we are dead."

"You are not dead Sebastian," Victor said and sat on a chair beside him. He mulled over whether to divulge his identity or indulge in the boy's delusion.

No grandfather had been mentioned. *Was there still one of them out there? If he had the physical appearance of an elderly man then what on earth was his age?* He wanted to know about the grandfather. "No, I am not your grandfather, Sebastian. However, he is safe with us."

Sebastian frowned and then cackled, "No, if you are not he, then you do not have my grandfather, for no one can capture my grandfather."

"You would be surprised at the success the Nazi army have at capturing people."

Sebastian spat a wad of bloody phlegm on the ground, "Fucking Nazi bastards."

"I'm sure your grandfather wouldn't want to hear such foul language coming from his grandson."

"Ha, you haven't met my grandfather."

"Well, maybe you should put matters right then? Maybe the man we have is the wrong man," Victor continued to bluff, "tell me about your grandfather."

The boy laughed and closed his eyes.

Victor thought he had succumbed to the cocktail of sedatives and had fallen unconscious; but then he spoke, "My grandfather is dead. My father killed him when we were just pups."

Victor tried to hide the excitement from his voice, this could be the answer he was after, nevertheless, his voice faltered, "How? How did your father kill your grandfather?"

Sebastian squinted, fighting the grogginess of the drugs, "Only three ways to kill a werewolf, fire, the tooth or claw of another werewolf, and silver."

"Silver?"

It was common knowledge among fanatics of the weird and macabre that mythological creatures like vampires and werewolves were vulnerable to this precious metal but Victor thought that was all nonsense, the stuff of fairy-tales. He also thought that of the thing in front of him.

He questioned Sebastian further, "Tell me about your grandfather."

Sebastian smiled, maybe glad of an audience, "My grandfather Peter Schäfer, the illegitimate son of Peter Stumpp, the werewolf of Bedburg."

Victor read about Stumpp, a German infamous in the sixteenth century, for being an incestuous cannibal and serial killer. He claimed, but it was never proven, that he was a werewolf.

He was executed over three hundred years ago.

Though Victor queried the truth of Sebastian's story he let the child continue talking.

"Father said there was madness in the family that came from that monster. Grandfather was a good man; he protected his pack. There were more of us then. But the local farmers grew tired of the lazier members feeding on livestock, they knew of our kind, knew we were secretive and only killed for food. They were angry and sought our kind out. They captured the youngest, easiest members of the pack so the adults would surrender. My father and his brother were captured. Grandfather Peter had enough.

"Enough of our people had been taken, men, women and children alike, and lashed to stakes to be burnt all night. He found out where they had my father and slaughtered them all but not before a lucky archer shot him with an arrow tipped in silver." Sebastian told his story with gusto. "The arrow pierced his brain but only slightly for the shot came from far, not enough propulsion, see? He carried my father away, he found him lying beside his dead brother, they had cut off his head and burned it. Grandfather returned home to his pack, before collapsing. The women cared for him, did everything they could but the silver either poisoned his brain or his own father's madness had been passed down and awoken. Grandfather Peter was a different man and began to commit atrocities much like his father, stealing babes out of their cribs in the nearby towns and eating them, even in human form. The females of the pack were targeted because of a sudden new lust, he was feared. My father was older and with the lady who would become my mother. They knew their existence was becoming threatened by grandfather's activities. My parents fled with my grandfather, my father built our house and cared for my grandfather as long as he could. But it wasn't long before Grandfather molested my mother and after she fell pregnant with me and Gretchen, Father feared for even more lives. My father cut off my grandfather's head with a silver sword he secretly fashioned, much like the way the villagers murdered his own brother and burnt him to ashes."

7.

Sebastian's story was astonishing whether it could be proven or not was irrelevant. Victor knew he had to test the silver method. If it was true, these creatures were vulnerable but he needed to keep the information to himself.

From then on he carried his journal everywhere, it held all information about his talks with the family, the possible secret of their death.

But how can I kill Christoph Schäfer, as Liebermann wanted, *without giving the Nazis the werewolf's final secret?*

It is common knowledge in myths and legends that werewolves are susceptible to the precious metal but that was all they were supposed to be - myth and legend.

Victor could put this to the test once.

God knows what Liebermann would do when he found out their weakness. Probably force them to fight, they were too precious to wipe out. He would force brother onto sister to create a truer lycan.

What mutations would occur then?

Victor spent nearly every waking moment beside Gwen in their rooms vigorously going over notes and calculations and how he could get this family out of the Nazis' clutches.

Dead or alive.

How can I humanely murder them and prevent the Nazis from creating a super army?

Victor was under Liebermann's constant watch, all his physical experiments on the father had ceased, he found out all he could short of opening the man's skull. He knew that what was next, if he couldn't find out a way to kill them he would have to completely dismantle Christoph Schäfer like an automobile engine, labelling each part and marking any changes or progress.

What would happen if that didn't kill the man?

Surely that would do the trick?

Fantastical as this species is, he didn't expect dismembered limbs to reattach.

He wished he had more time but knew the sudden workload on top of his wife's care, at his age, meant it would be the straw that broke the camel's back regarding his own good health.

Why can't the bastards just leave us alone?

They never gave him a choice.

They destroyed their home, the home they lived in since marriage, and brought them here to this hell hole on a rumour.

Victor's epiphany came when he reread his notes on Sebastian and the concoction of drugs used to subdue him.

He administered the serum by injection.

If he upped the strength accordingly there was no reason to believe it wouldn't put the boy into a temporary catatonic state.

He would administer a large dose of silver nitrate into the boy's system.

He could adopt this method for the parents.

A large part of him longed to find a way to release the family back into the secrecy they kept for so long.

He was certain the boy may be troublesome as he grew older, that his underlying mental health issues would worsen, but he was sure the parents and sister would deal with that.

8.

Victor unlocked Christoph Schäfer's metal cuffs and secreted the key in his jacket pocket.

He looked deep and mournfully at the big man's face; a mutual understanding passed between them. They understood the risks they were about to take.

Christoph Schäfer smiled sadly. "Thank you."

That morning while Victor worked in the laboratory testing the doctored serum against the blood samples Liebermann lost his temper and tore apart Victor's rooms, convinced the elderly doctor was hiding something. Gwen received the brunt of the madman's temper, he left her bruised in her own filth. When Victor returned to this scene of abuse he changed his plans.

He left his wife in the care of one of the nurses that occasionally helped and went to put his plan into action.

"Come Sebastian, the moment I told you about has arrived," Victor said to the boy on the bed. Over the last few days, as he hoped, the boy began to trust him and not so much sedation was required for his visits.

"Will I need to have an injection again?" Sebastian whined as Victor unfastened the cuffs which bound his wrists and ankles. Victor found it comical that someone who went through from man to werewolf was frightened by a needle. "Yes, but not yet, only when you're with your sister," Victor said nervously and took the boy's cold hand in his.

He led the boy across the room, his cane clicked against the floor, "Now we wait a few moments."

Christoph closed his eyes and focused on the creature within.

Intense concentration was necessary to use the wolf's powers for manipulating the anatomical make up of his inner ear and strengthening his hearing.

He knew in another room not far away his wife would be doing the same.

As his hearing became the wolf's he detected more sound in the building. Like tuning a radio he ignored the noises and voices that didn't concern him and listened for only one.

Victor's.

"Now we wait a few moments."

A strangled cry came from Christoph.

He forced his werewolf to the surface quicker than he had ever done in his life, his skin burst like a blood-filled balloon as the bones and muscles destroyed one body to build another.

His heart felt like it would rupture in the seconds it took for him to change but by the time the guards outside the room had struggled with the door he was all werewolf.

Three guards ran into the room, calling behind for back-up.

They open-fired immediately.

Though their bullets wouldn't be very effective they were still surprised how the gunshot barely slowed the massive ruddy red werewolf charging towards them.

Christoph hit them like a locomotive, completely crushing one of the men into the wall beside the opened door. The other two guards turned to flee but he snatched at their heads with his bear-like paws and squeezed them like overripe fruit.

Another guard jumped in through the doorway, Christoph ploughed the opening sending brick, mortar, blood and bone in all directions.

Somewhere close by an alarm sounded followed by shooting.

Victor opened Sebastian's cell door and stood aside, ashen-faced as several soldiers pounded the hallway towards the sound of gunfire. He waited until they passed to spirit the boy away.

An almighty roar echoed from the opposite end of the hallway; his mother's werewolf was tearing the soldiers apart.

He knew her beast-call.

Sebastian cried, "Mother!"

Victor pulled the boy towards him, "It's okay, you'll be with her soon. We have to get your sister first."

Agatha Schäfer raked at armed soldiers and ignored the hot lances of their bullets.
She would do anything to save her family.
She heard her husband roar and bounded through the corridors to find him.

Liberman growled with exertion as he sprinted towards the commotion, half a dozen men jogged behind him in fireproof clothing. Each man weighed down with a fuel tank and flamethrower.

The man and woman escaped.

Liebermann spotted them immediately in the mess hall, tables being overturned as they tried to reach one another. They were surrounded by dozens of soldiers who covered them with automatic fire.

Christoph batted the soldiers out of his way and thanked his luck that no shots had struck his head. Although he could regenerate at speed he was still flesh and blood, there were too many bullets.

He could feel himself slowing, the injuries were too frequent for his body to recover, all it would take is a headshot to completely disorientate him and they would take him down.

He ducked and charged at the wooden dining tables, making them flip up and simultaneously shield him and push the soldiers out of his way like a snow plough.

Agatha knew she couldn't keep this up much longer, there were too many men.

Her husband was a mess of red matted bloodied fur. He bashed his way towards her, one arm almost severed through the multitude of gunshots.

She struck out at those in her path and was mere feet away when she felt the double zip of two shots to the back of her huge triangular head.

Numbness immediately disabled her left side and she crashed into the tables.

She heard her husband's outburst as her vision faded.

Christoph watched her fall; the tables collapsed beneath her weight as she rolled over onto the floor.

His left arm swung uselessly, he knew it would soon be over, he gave one last burst of energy and leapt towards Agatha.

He held her to his chest and turned his back on the soldiers' bullets.

Agatha slowly changed back to human form; her naked broken body riddled with bullet holes. She was missing fingers, her internal organs were destroyed, wheezing came from ragged holes in her chest.

The headshots exited from the top of her head had blown the majority of her hair and scalp away.

In time the lycanthropy could heal that but Christoph knew time was something they had run out of.

He clutched her to his chest, engulfed her in his massive animal bulk and howled towards the ceiling.

Liebermann beckoned his men on; the parents were dispensable, all that mattered were the children. The children were the future, "Surround them and burn them!"

The flamethrower team lined up close to the Schäfers, Christoph had given up, he was back to human form.

Agatha managed to fight back the black veil of unconsciousness long enough to see flickers of flamethrowers flames reflected in Christoph's eyes.

Liebermann shouted fire and they were immolated in each other's arms.

9.

Victor tucked his cane under his arm and held the children's hands.

They walked away from the screaming and shooting.

Sebastian looked back in hatred and fear, Gretchen clutched the old man, weeping uncontrollably.

"You have to trust me, everything will be fine," Victor repeated over and over again as he led them to a room at the end of a deserted corridor.

He ushered them into the room without haste and locked it behind him.

Metal gurneys, the operating theatre, Victor pointed towards a large, unbarred window. "Gretchen, quick, get up there and try to open that window."

The girl wiped her face on her sleeve and pushed one of the gurneys over to the wall beneath the window before leaping up. She pushed her palms against the glass and the window slowly began to move.

She grunted with effort until a little of her inner beast's strength kicked in and helped her slam the window up. She turned back to Victor when she heard Sebastian yelp.

Victor stood over him; Sebastian jolted on the floor like he was being electrocuted.

"What's wrong with him?" Gretchen screamed and jumped to her brother's aid.

Victor was dumbfounded.

Gretchen crouched by her brother's side and held his shoulders to stop him from moving during his fit, his fingers curled into claws.

The tendons in his neck strained as his head stretched back. Just the whites of his eyes showed, all the veins in his forehead, temples, face and neck throbbed and stood out like grey tinged lightning.

Victor's hand lit on her shoulder and she pressed her face to it for comfort.

"I'm so sorry Lady Esmeralda," Victor said quietly.

Gretchen turned her face upwards in time to see Victor lower the syringe, press it into her neck and inject the serum.

Victor threw in the Schafers' blood and tissue samples after he gave the children to the incinerator. He left the window open in the incinerator room and staggered down the corridor towards his rooms. He was exhausted and knew it wouldn't take Liebermann long to find out what he had done.

He didn't care about the consequences.

Ahead soldiers brought two more metal gurneys with blackened corpses towards the incinerator.

There was one more thing left for Victor to do.

10.

His heart beat in synchrony with the sound of the heavy boots.

"Gwen, they are almost here!" Victor said and took the matches from her hands and lit the contents of the metal bin. The flame reacted quickly with the lighter fluid he poured over the leather journal. The dry pages curled and burned. Gwen sat in the same spot in her armchair blackened after her attack. The nurse patched her up and left before the shooting began.

"Oh Victor, look. Isn't it beautiful?" She pointed a swollen hand over their ruined room towards the fireplace though she was seeing something from a long time ago.

Voices screamed his name, strong fists pounded against the thick door.

Shoulders replaced fists and the door exploded inwards.

Men in long black leather coats stormed into the small space, a select few soldiers accompanied, their guns aimed at Victor. Liebermann saw the documents burning and sneered.

"You think I believe you would have destroyed all your work?"

"It's all gone, I swear it. Every last trace."

Liebermann stared at him, he didn't think he was lying, he was trained in detection. He turned to the nearest soldier, "Shoot the woman."

The soldier, barely eighteen, raised his weapon and without hesitation, fired.

Victor screamed and jumped in front of his wife; the bullet struck him in the centre of his chest.

Victor lay on his side, blood gushed from the hole. Liebermann gave a signal to the soldiers and they fired again.

Gwen shook, a sickening samba, as the bullets peppered her torso.

FUR

[a preview]

MATTHEW CASH

Prologue

Danny stepped onto the snow. His running shoes offered little protection against the ice. The snow had fallen all weekend without letting up. He yanked on the drawstring of his hoodie and headed towards the canal.

Although Danny was going his usual way to school he had no intention of getting there. It was a waste of time. He could read and write and do basic math, why bother with anything else?

There were no aspirations amongst him and his friends other than getting to the age where they could be paid for doing nothing. Boxford was a dead end, not even big enough to merit being called a town. The closest jobs would be in the next town, Sudbury, or the industrial park in between, and he wasn't going to work in a fucking shop or factory.

He came off the path and started down the brick slope which led to the canal towpath and skidded down the smooth tiled sides.

The canal was frozen solid; the only way you could tell where the path ended and the canal began was the slight variants in the depth of the snow.

A shopping trolley sat motionless on the ice, Danny smirked and wondered if it had been one of his mates who dumped it there.

Whilst thinking of his surrogate family he noticed the music before he rounded the bend.

He could see the huddled shapes of his potential crew; one he hoped to be part of. To be a member of the GMC was his only aspiration.

That was his vocation, and with the shoplifting and petty vandalism already started he was getting the work experience. When he showed up at school he sold some of the stolen gear to his fellow pupils.

"Here comes Fannyboy," Neep jeered when he saw Danny duck beneath the low bridge. The others; four other lads from the estate laughed and swarmed, pelting him with back-slaps and fist-bumps, their usual greetings.

"What's up?" He nodded to Neep, their current elected leader. Nephew of one of the estate's older hard men and had use of his uncle's contacts.

Neep grinned showing teeth that were Crooked and chipped from fighting. DIY tattoos adorned his face and neck; stars, daggers, twin savage Pitbulls each side of his throat. "Uncle Charlie's due in a bit with some quality shit."

"Nice one," Danny said grinning, wishing the older boy would be a bit more specific on what the *quality shit* was. "I gotta go to fucking school. Do you want me to take anything?"

Neep looked aghast, then nudged the lad to his left and winked, "See, this kid is conscientious. Offering to do work for us? He's a good man, ain't you Dan?"

Danny shrugged.

Bailey, a tall youth, grinned, reached forward and yanked on Danny's school tie.

"Hey Danny, is your brother still taking it up the shitter?" said Motto, adding his trademark annoying cackle.

He was a skinny, greasy, pimply boy, not much older than Danny. Danny wasn't keen on the lad, didn't trust him at all, but was pretty sure he could take him in a fight. "As far as I know, Michael," Danny said, knowing how much Motto hated being called by his real name, "but I'll be sure to pass on your interest to him."

Motto's smile vanished and he took a defensive step forward, further enraged by the other four gang members' laughter and congratulating Danny on his comeback.

Neep put a hand on each of their bellies, "now, now ladies, we're all friends here right?"

"Right," Danny nodded.

Motto was reluctant. Neep shoved his face against his staring him down, "Right, Michael?"

Motto nodded slowly, "Yeah, right."

"Right," Neep said happily, "if you can give it, you should be able to take it and all."

"Just like my brother," Danny muttered.

The whole gang joined in with this joke and Neep grabbed him in an affectionate headlock and ruffled his hair. "Man, I love this kid, fucking cracks me up no end."

Pyro and Benson, two big brutish boys, one with a liking for arson, exchanged glances at something that caught their eye.

Pyro poked Neep. "Neep, check who's coming down the path."

The boys all turned in the direction Danny came in, expecting to see a couple of the girls from the estate, or maybe a rival gang from the next town. But all they could see was a black-clad figure walking gingerly over the nearby bridge; a red bus passed as he turned into the slope to the towpath.

"That's that old Nazi prick," Motto said, they all knew the man's distinctive frame.

He stood at the top of the slope like he was having second thoughts about risking the descent.

"Ah, he won't come down here," Neep said as they watched him, "can't believe the old bastard's out. Don't they have fucking Ring and Ride where he lives?"

"Old bastard could afford his own bloody chauffeur," Motto scowled. They continued to watch as the figure started down and vanished out of sight.

Silence befell the group as they looked at their leader with surprise.

After almost a minute of nobody saying anything they heard the old man's walking stick tapping on the ice as he walked across the treacherous surface to the obscuring bend in the path.

Danny felt a wave of nausea and unease wash over him and to stop his hands from shaking busied himself with smartening his school tie and uniform.

Due to the Village Hall reconstruction the footpath beside it was out of bounds. Virtually everyone who lived on that side of the village would rather take the extra ten-minute walk through the Green Man housing estate than take the canal towpath. Unsavoury types, usually the younger delinquent generation, raised in one of the Green Man estate's five multi-storey tower blocks, frequented the towpath.

Victor Krauss, a ninety year-old native of Germany and the wealth behind the Village Hall restoration, pushed his cane into the ground and started carefully down the sloped steps. The cold weather made his joints ache and the snow increased this; however, there was no way he was going to be intimidated by the prospect of ruffians.

Standing by the frozen water he filled his lungs with the cleansing cold air, pulled the furred flaps of his deerstalker over his ears and strode confidentially along. He stopped when he rounded the bend and saw the group of kids; well, they were kids to him anyway, before the bridge. He considered turning around and forcing himself to take the bus, or leave it until another day.

There were at least half a dozen of them laughing and jostling one another. Music, if you could call it that blared from their mobile devices, they talked, or rather shouted over it.

Victor continued to walk, he was too old and stubborn to let intimidation show, he survived the Second World War.

He met bloodthirsty Nazis who were pure evil; these children wouldn't last a minute if they met one of the SS. But those were evil men, these were just bored youths with nothing better to do. One was in a school uniform for Heaven's sake.

He faked confidence and continued, careful not to lose footing on the icy ground. They ceased all chatter when he approached and eyed one another with conspiratorial sneers.

Victor nodded to them and smiled. He went through the small group beneath the bridge.

He passed one of them and stepped into the gloom beneath the bridge when he felt a hand tap him on the shoulder.

"Yo, Grandad, you got the time?"

Victor turned to the big kid who asked the time. He smiled at the youth and rolled his sleeve up. "Yes, of course, dear boy. It's almost nine o'clock."

The boy grunted, "Cheers."

Victor nodded and turned to leave.

"Give us your wallet!"

Hell was unleashed beneath the bridge.

Shrieks pierced the frosted morning air and a murderous bloodbath began.

Holy shit. Holy shit. Holy fucking shit. Danny slid across the icy brick pathway, he curved to the left to stop himself slipping from the towpath and through the ice into the canal. It may have been thick enough to hold his weight but he wasn't prepared to find out. He knew he had probably ruined all chances of joining the Green Man Crew now but there was no way he was going to stay whilst they mugged the old guy.

Danny half-ran, half-skidded across the slippery path, he could hear the old man's raised voice. His German lilt sounded like the Nazis in the old films his dad watched.

His lungs burned with heavy exertion and the sharp, cold air.

Other smaller bridges spanned the canal path.

He took refuge under an old footbridge.

A sudden loud crack came from the way he had come. He wondered if Neep had a gun; he had bragged about guns before, but it was soon followed by the sounds of splashing.

"Oh, fucking hell." Danny thought, he felt his bladder leak, images of Neep hurting the old man before pushing him into the sub-zero water sickened him. *Will I be an accessory to murder?* The wet walls and piss smell didn't register as he squeezed into a corner. He hunched and vomited everything he had eaten that morning, every part-digested cornflake was spat onto the steaming, stinking heap at his feet.

Danny knew he needed to move, he got to his feet. If Neep and the others came this way he would be bound to get it in the heck for running off on them.

He started moving, *fuck school, fuck the lot of them.* He wouldn't feel safe until he was shut in his bedroom back at his dad's, and even then the fact that he was slap bang in the middle of the estate meant that he would never truly feel safe after this. Whatever repercussions that would follow would be his to bear.

His dad called for him at dinner time.

There was no chance he would be able to stomach the grease his father had whacked together but knew his dad wouldn't quit hollering until he made an appearance.

Danny didn't want to leave his room. He had been there all day since the incident; he could do without added grief off his dad for wasting food, even though the fat old wanker would eat it if he left it. His dad still cooked for three of them even though Tony refused to eat his cooking. Danny's brother was health-conscious and prepared his own food.

His father screamed for him again, this time there was something additional to his usual irritation. Danny slammed open his bedroom door and headed to the kitchen but saw his dad in the lounge staring at the television. Danny's blood ran cold as he inched into the room and saw the familiar stretch of canal on the local news.

Headlines scrolled across the lower screen as the newsreader went through the details. The headline confused him and he retched up a throat full of bile.

DOG ATTACK KILLS FIVE

1.

Colleen Cassidy teased her fingertips beneath the raw pastry on the flour-covered tabletop just as the phone rang.

"Jesus wept," she cursed, her accent still retained some of its stateside origins.

Undeterred by the phone's intrusion she continued with the delicate artistry of placing the lid on the dish before her.

A terracotta bowl filled to the brim with steak, onions, mushrooms and a few twists of the salt grinder was swathed in a pastry blanket.

The phone stopped ringing.

"Probably a sales call," Colleen said to a fat ginger tom cat sat at her feet awaiting any dropped morsels. Colleen wiped away a blonde curl with the back of a wrist and set about crimping the pie lid to the base. Satisfied with her handiwork, she plucked a decorative leaf she cut out of spare pastry and stuck it on the top. Micky always had to have the leaf, bless him.

The youngest of her boys, Micky, was still her baby although he was nearly seventeen. She had done her best being a single parent but they threw their labels at him growing up regardless.

Autism, ADHD, whatever, he was her baby, he worked hard at the supermarket, people knew he was simple but they also knew not to mock that.

He was the best of the bunch, Micky.

She thought of her other boys as she loaded the second pie into the oven. They would storm in here, eat her out of house and home then be away again until the next time they got hungry.

But at least Micky stayed.

Billy, Jake and Robert would only end up in trouble; prison, or dead like their father, she cast her mind back over a decade when her long-term partner was taken from her by the law.

Nathaniel was trying to provide for his family the only way he knew how; theft. A robbery completely fluffed, his brother got him a shotgun, she told him never to get involved with guns.

An old country song she hadn't thought about in years echoed throughout an imagined memory of the event she didn't bear witness to. *Don't take your guns to town*, the singer warned, Nathaniel Neeper, gunned down by the police. God knew what went wrong, probably the fact that he was born that way. *Leave your guns at home.*

Colleen wiped a tear and flour streaked her cheek like war paint. She still had an old photo of him stuck on the wall, Nathaniel and Charles Neeper, two peas in a pod, well-toned, fag packets tucked under the sleeves of their polo shirts.

They thought were the modern equivalent to Ronnie and Reggie Kray.

Nathaniel had been so handsome, Robert was just like him, apart from his mean streak, Charlie was now a reminder of the man Nathan might have been.

She turned her eye to Nathan's slightly younger brother Charlie, if Robert found out they were seeing each other he would be livid. He held onto the memory of his father like he was some kind of hero.

Every boyfriend she had since the boy hit twelve had been driven away. Her last man, a decent fella for a change, had a job and everything, woke up in bed one morning with Robert pressing a knife to his throat.

She didn't think that would happen if he found out about her and Charlie. They helped one another out. That's how they put it but she knew what they were up to, well, at least some of it. She never went without.

"My boys," Colleen said looking at the photo of the two brothers but thinking about the boys Nathaniel left behind.

Ten minutes later, whilst she dug out the recipe for Micky's favourite pudding, a hammering came from the door, and the pies, like her eldest son, were completely ruined.

Red.

Thick, clotting, bulbous clumps like rubies dripped from the knife with a messy wet splatter onto the smooth surface.

"Oh, Herbert you are such a clumsy oaf!" Ethel said as she took the knife from Herbert's liver-spotted hand. "Let me do it for you." She wiped up the strawberry jam with a napkin, rested it folded on the side of his plate and spread the contents of a small pot on Herbert's fruit scone.

Herbert chuckled; his spherical bald head shook with embarrassment. "I don't know what I would do without you, Ethel."

Ethel patted his hand and she smiled at him. "It's alright; there are some things we women are just better at."

Since his wife died three years previous Herbert spent most of his time at the shops, in particular, the café. It was where his friends were, this was the local haunt for the nearly-dead.

That's how he referred to this band of geriatric widows and widowers.

He took a bite from the scone and jam, happy that Rebecca got the smooth kind, there were no strawberry pips to get under the plates of his false teeth. He rolled his eyes comically behind thick-lensed glasses with enthusiastic pleasure. "Oh, that hits the spot."

Ethel poured a cup of tea for herself and without thinking one for Herbert too. It was funny how things turned out for her.

She was married twice, both to well-off men, but they both died of heart attacks. She was often lonely at her house; it was far too big for her and since her legs started playing up she stopped using upstairs. The social gathering in the supermarket café had become a regular thing now, and she even admitted to looking forward to seeing the others. It was strange, but she supposed it was just the way things were, that those who had been coming here for years seemed to have paired off with one another.

She peered over her cup at Herbert as he stared out of the window across the street. She had been like a surrogate wife to him for two years but there was no intimacy in their friendship beyond the odd peck on the cheek, they were too old for that nonsense. She believed men of that generation needed looking after and in the same context women of her generation needed someone to look after.

"Oh-oh," Herbert said smacking his palm on the table and cocking a thumb out the window, "here they come, Dr Strangelove and Bob Marley."

Always says the same thing every day, Ethel thought, *I wonder what he was like as a young man? Probably the same but less wrinkled*, she stifled laughter. Herbert had alopecia and was completely bald; she always thought he resembled a little pink Brussel sprout; with glasses.

"Morning, Ethel, hello Herbert," a voice came from behind them. They turned to greet their other friend Elizabeth.

Elizabeth looked like an ageing starlet. Debonair good looks and cheekbones that would have made her beautiful back in her day. A pitter-patter of excited feet always accompanied her wherever she went. Her dog Frankie.

Elizabeth took off her coat and looked mournfully over at the two people behind the serving counter. "Oh Rebecca, darling, you don't mind if Frankie comes inside do you? It's so gosh darn cold outside."

Bex reluctantly nodded. "Just make sure he behaves himself."

Elizabeth sat and the little two-toned dog paddled its front legs up against her knee. "No, you stay down there, baby. Be a good boy." Frankie slid under the table and rested at her feet.

The horrific carnage was described in far more detail than on the evening news the day before., the newspaper expanded on the 'ferocious dog attack' angle. Interviews with the RSPCA explained how there would be a strict rule in the vicinity about keeping all dogs on leashes. A dog warden van would be patrolling the town on the lookout for the dangerous dogs.

Danny caught snippets of information from the exhausted glance he took from his dad's paper that morning.

Headlines on the sandwich board outside the newsagents simply read 'TEEN DOG MASSACRE'.

He surprised his father by actually going to school that morning. For the first time in forever, his dad suggested he might want to take the day off.

He saw Danny had been hit hard by the news, knowing that he knew the kids in question. The only ones on the news who were named were the oldest of the five killed.

When his dad came home from his daily drink at the local he told Danny the names of the others killed. All it did was confirm what he already knew and Danny cried into his pillow all night.

Danny walked past a couple of shops on what folk in vast exaggeration referred to as the high street. He stopped when he heard a familiar clicking approaching.

He pressed himself into the alcove of a shuttered bookie and fumbled on his phone, lowering his face.

He couldn't believe the old German guy was up and about after his ordeal.

There were forever stories of old people going down hill after such incidents, like the psychological trauma of such an event caused them to sink into a life of petrified hermitage.

Danny risked a quick glimpse, the tall man was wrapped in a winter overcoat, scarf and hat, and seemed unfazed by anything. His face, though aged and lined, bore no tell-tale signs of any recent stresses. Danny turned into the doorway to further avoid recognition as the old German walked past.

He wondered how he managed to avoid the dogs.

"Here they are!" Herbert shouted as the two men whom he referred to as Dr Strangelove and Bob Marley walked into the café.

"Morning all," Norman said from his wheelchair and waved regally like he was the Queen. His full head of grey hair was coiffed to perfection.

The one Herbert called Bob Marley was an elderly Jamaican whose name was Trevor. He pushed Norman's wheelchair over to the serving counter and grinned. "Wogwan T-Dog," he shouted in his strong Jamaican accent and held out a fist towards the man serving like he saw his grandchildren do.

Tony was a young stereotypical gay man; with bright bleached hair and a perpetually flamboyant exterior.

He bumped his small hand against Trevor's and prepared the new customers' usual orders.

"How's it hanging Herbie boy?" Trevor said, sighing loudly as he took a seat after parking Norman at the table.

Herbert put his teacup down, "Well it used to stand and watch me pick my nose, but now it drools upon my toes!"

Trevor roared with his infamous laughter. One of those raucous laughs that never failed to make people smile. He clapped the little bald man on the shoulder and laughed some more.

"Morning ladies," Norman said, making conversation with Ethel and Elizabeth and slipped a hand under the table to pet Frankie. "I must say that you both look ravishing today."

He grinned; tobacco-stained teeth and whisky-breath.

Elizabeth held a hand to her nose, "Oh Norman, you've not been on the whisky already?"

Norman recoiled in his wheelchair, "Aye, I might have had a wee dram on my porridge this morning, medicinal purposes, to warm my cockles on such a bitter day."

Ethel grimaced but couldn't fault Norman for his vices, everybody had them.

"You're a stereotype Scotsman, Norman, whisky drinking, porridge eating and..."

"Permanently legless," Norman said and slapped his legs which ended at the knees.

Ethel let a snort of laughter escape before stifling it. "I was going to say," she watched as he poured coins into his palm from a small leather pouch and counted the change, to hand to Trevor, "tight-fisted."

"Tight-fisted?" Norman said, his booming Scottish accent echoed throughout the café, "I'll have you know that I bought Trevor no fewer than three pints of ale yesterday!"

Trevor stopped in mid-conversation with Herbert. "Yeah man and you still owe me another two from last week!" Again, the contagious laughter followed.

Before the old friends could spend the next thirty minutes arguing about who owed who Ethel changed the subject. "I wonder if Victor will show," she said to no one in particular, a thought out loud.

Elizabeth was in her line of vision so took it to reply, "He'll not show that poor, poor man."

The men went sullen at their friend's name being mentioned.

"I still can't believe that people would be so cruel," Trevor said, all traces of humour gone from his voice.

"I went to see him at the hospital," Herbert smiled sadly, "they were amazed it didn't kill him."

"Ach, he's a tough man, our Victor, fought hard for his country just like some of our men did, even though he knew that the mad Austrian bastard was nuts. He'll shake this off like it was nothing," Norman said confidently.

"I wish I had your optimism Norman," Ethel said, peering into her teacup.

Norman chuckled, "It's no optimism hen, he's now coming into the café."

Ethel and the others gasped before they heard the clicking of his walking-stick against the flooring of the café.

Elizabeth's dog growled lowly in its throat before whining and lying down behind her legs.

Everyone apart from Norman turned as Victor marched up to the counter.

"Rebecca my dear, a coffee at your convenience please," Victor said, dabbing a gingham handkerchief to his nose. He scrutinized the others from the corners of pale blue eyes. "Please, put your tongues back in your mouths, I am not a ghost, nor will I pose for photographs."

A twinkle of the German's dry sense of humour sparkled in his eyes as he steadily walked over to join them at the tables. He sat carefully and slowly crossed his right leg over the left. He pulled off thick gloves and removed his fur-lined hat.

Nobody said anything until Bex placed steaming black coffee before him and a hand on his shoulder. Victor pursed his wrinkled lips and sipped the coffee, he took his time, knew all eyes were on him.

Bex broke the silence, "Good to see you up and about Victor."

Victor nodded and focused his attention on the stares of his friends. "Well, which one of you is going to start firing the questions first?"

About Matthew Cash

Matthew Cash, or Matty-Bob Cash as he is known to most, was born and raised in Suffolk, which is the setting for his debut novel *Pinprick*.

He is compiler and editor of *Death by Chocolate*, a chocoholic horror anthology and the *12Days: STOCKING FILLERS* anthology.

In 2016, he launched his own publishing house, Burdizzo Books, and took shit-hot editor and author Em Dehaney on board to keep him in shape, and together they brought into existence *SPARKS*: an electrical horror anthology, *The Reverend Burdizzo's Hymn Book, Under the Weather*, Visions from the Void ***, and *The Burdizzo Mix Tape Vol. 1.* He has numerous solo releases on Kindle and several collections in paperback.

Originally, with Burdizzo Books, the intention was to compile charity anthologies a few times a year but his creation has grown into something so much more powerful *insert mad laughter here*.

He is currently working on numerous projects; his third novel, *FUR*, was launched in 2018.

*With *Back Road Books*
** With Jonathan Butcher

He has been writing stories since he first learned to write and most, although not all, tend to slip into the multi-layered murky depths of the horror genre.

His influences (from when he first started reading to present-day) are, to name but a small, select few: Roald Dahl, James Herbert, Clive Barker, Stephen King, Stephen Laws, and more recently, he enjoys Adam Nevill, F.R Tallis, Michael Bray, Gary Fry, William Meikle and Iain Rob Wright (who featured Matty-Bob in his famous *A-Z of Horror* title *M is For Matty-Bob*, plus Matthew wrote his version of events, which was included as a bonus). He is a father of two, a husband of one, and a zookeeper of numerous fur babies.

You can find him here:
www.facebook.com/pinprickbymatthewcash
https://www.amazon.co.uk/-/e/B010MQTWKK
www.burdizzobooks.com

Other Releases by Matthew Cash

Novels:

Virgin and The Hunter
Pinprick
FUR

Novellas:

Ankle Biters
KrackerJack
Illness
Clinton Reed's FAT
Hell And Sebastian
Waiting for Godfrey
Deadbeard
The Cat Came Back
KrackerJack 2
Demon Thingy [with Jonathan Butcher]
Werwolf
Frosty
Keida-in-the-flames
Tesco a-go-go

Short Stories

Why Can't I Be You?
Slugs and Snails and Puppydog Tails
Oldtimers
Hunt The C*nt

Anthologies compiled and edited by Matthew Cash:

Death by Chocolate
12 Days: STOCKING FILLERS
12 Days: 2016 Anthology
12 Days: 2017 [with Em Dehaney]
The Reverend Burdizzo's Hymn Book (with Em Dehaney)
Sparks [with Em Dehaney]
Visions from the Void [with Jonathan Butcher]
Under the Weather
Welcome to a town called Hell
Burdizzo Mix Tape Volume 1
Corona-Nation Street
Beneath the Leaves

Anthologies Featuring Matthew Cash

Rejected for Content 3: Vicious Vengeance
JEApers Creepers
Full Moon Slaughter
Down the Rabbit Hole: Tales of Insanity

Collections
The Cash Compendium Volume 1
The Cash Compendium Continuity

Websites:
www.Facebook.com/pinprickbymatthewcash

www.burdizzobooks.com

Pinprick
Matthew Cash

All villages have their secrets, and Brantham is no different.

Twenty years ago, after foolish risk-taking turned into tragedy, Shane left the rural community under a cloud of suspicion and rumour. Events from that night remained unexplained, memories erased, questions unanswered. Now a notorious politician, he returns to his birthplace when the offer from a property developer is too good to decline.

With big plans to haul Brantham into the 21st century, the developers have already made a devastating impact on the once-quaint village.

But then the headaches begin, followed by the nightmarish visions.

Soon Shane wishes he had never returned, as Brantham reveals its ugly secret.

Virgin and The Hunter
Matthew Cash

Hi, I'm God. And I have a confession to make.

I live with my two best friends and the girl of my dreams, Persephone. When the opportunity knocks, we are usually down the pub having a few drinks, or we'll hang out in Christchurch Park until it gets dark, then go home to do college stuff. Even though I struggle a bit financially, life is good, carefree.

Well, it was.

Things have started going downhill recently, from the moment I started killing people.

KrackerJack
Matthew Cash

Five people wake up in a warehouse, bound to chairs. Before each of them, tacked to the wall are their witness testimonies.

They each played a part in labelling one of Britain's most loved family entertainers a paedophile and sex offender.

Clearly, revenge is the reason they have been brought here, but the man they accused is supposed to be dead.

Opportunity knocks and Diddy Dave Diamond has one last game show to host—and it's a knockout.

Krackerjack2
Matthew Cash

Ever wondered what would happen if a celebrity faked their own death and decided they had changed their minds?

Two years ago, publicly-shunned comedian Diddy Dave Diamond convinced the nation that he was dead, only to return from beyond the grave to seek retribution on those who ruined his career and tainted his legacy.

Innocent or not, only one person survived Diddy Dave Diamond's last-ever game show, but the forfeit prize was imprisonment for similar alleged crimes.

Prison is not kind to inmates with those types of convictions, as the sole survivor finds out, but there's a sudden glimmer of hope.

Someone has surfaced in the public eye, claiming to be the dead comedian.

Fur
Matthew Cash

The old-aged pensioners of Boxford are set in their ways, loyal to each other and their daily routines. With families and loved ones either moved on to pastures new or maybe even the next life, these folks can become dependent on one another.

But what happens when the natural ailments of old age begin to take their toll? What if they were given the opportunity to heal and overcome the things that make everyday life less tolerable? What if they were given this ability without their consent?

When a group of local thugs attack the village's wealthy Victor Krauss, they unwittingly create a maelstrom of events that not only could destroy their home but everyone in and around it.

Are the old folk the cause or the cure of the horrors?

Also, from
Burdizzo Books:

The Children at The Bottom of The Gardden
Jonathan Butcher

At the edge of the coastal city of Seadon, there stands a dilapidated farmhouse, and at the back of the farmhouse there is a crowd of rotten trees, where something titters and calls.

The Gardden.

Its playful voice promises games, magic, wonders, lies – and roaring torrents of blood.

It speaks not just to its eccentric keeper, Thomas, but also to the outcasts and deviants from Seadon's criminal underworld.

At first, they are too distracted by their own tangled mistakes and violent lives to notice, but one-by-one they'll come: a restless Goth, a cheating waster, a sullen concubine, a perverted drug baron, and a murderous sociopath.

Haunted by shadowed things with coal-black eyes, something malicious and ancient will lure them ever-closer. And on a summer's day not long from now, they'll gather beneath the leaves in a place where nightmares become flesh, secrets rise up from the dark, and a voice coaxes them to play and stay, yes, yes, yes, forever.

The Little Exorcist
Alys Daddi

Molly's dad, Wayne, has always been a practical joker, a proper wind-up merchant, his sense of humour holds no bounds, and when what he thinks is a trick at his expense backfires, he is left feeling unusual.

Wayne's silliness stoops to new and more juvenile levels but strangely, he professes to having no recollection of this behaviour.

Things go from silly to strange when these events turn into regular blackouts and Wayne reveals secrets from his past that may have implications on his present-day mental health. With his family and friends trying to support him and come to terms with living with someone who may have Dissociative Identity or Multiple Personality Disorder, it's only his daughter Molly who wonders if there is more to his illness than the psychiatric team can deal with.

The Wassailers
Em Dehaney

This wickedly sinister Christmas poem by Em Dehaney is a traditional folk tale with a terrifying twist, warning of the dangers of modern greed and consumerism. Featuring pen-and-ink illustrations by Krzysztof Wroński that are dark, dense and dripping with old-world menace.

Burdizzo Books have brought the two together, along with a foreword by no other than the master of horror Graham Masterton, in this gruesome, yet gripping, unique festive nightmare.

Curl up by the fire, fill your cup with mulled wine, and pray The Wassailers don't knock on your door.